I0518185

JACLYN THE RIPPER

Was the Ripper a Woman?

CHAPTER ONE

1888 Whitechapel London

She sank into the bed as the man beside her began to groan, she wasn't half as exhausted as he was and what the hell was that stink coming from him?

"That was good Jaclyn, are you taking something new?" the man beside her asked.

"No I am not, it's the same old me," Jaclyn said, she was staring at the ceiling. She couldn't bear to face the man.

"How much do I owe you?" the man asked.

"You know how much Ben. It is the same price every time," Jaclyn shrugged.

She got out of the bed to grab her dress on the floor, she sat on the edge of the bed and held her head. She hated what she did, she hated that she was a source of pleasure to smelly men who frequented the streets of London. Most of the men she slept with were miners and men who cleaned the sewers.

Most of her business involved her staring at their face and their rotting teeth as she had sex with them. They paid her with peanuts, she made barely enough to get by every day.

Jaclyn felt a hand around her waist.

"You want to go another round Jaclyn?"

Jaclyn turned her neck at the man touching her. She felt repulsed as she saw him smile.

"No, Ben. I think I'm done for today," Jaclyn said, she held in her breathe, Ben stank.

"Oh come on Jaclyn, don't be a bum," Ben said.

"Ben, just pay me and I will be on my merry way."

Jaclyn stood and got dressed while the man stared at her.

"Your breasts are huge," Ben smiled at her.

'Oh God," Jaclyn thought, she was going to have a fit if she didn't get out of the stinking room.

"Just pay me Ben."

"Oh there is a problem with that," Ben sniffed. "I don't get me pay till next week."

"You fucker," Jaclyn exclaimed. "You said you got paid already. You came in here asking for one of the best girls that's why I came up with you," Jaclyn shouted.

"Oh come on Jaclyn, I wanted to get the fresh girls not the old rotten ones," Ben grinned showing his teeth. "What do you say we go one more and I owe you for next week?"

"Fuck off," Jaclyn said, she grabbed Ben's sock on the floor and threw it at him.

"Ow, what did you do that for?"

"You better have my money by next week or I will cut your balls off," Jaclyn spat. "Don't think I am joking Ben."

Jaclyn packed her dress around her body and turned to leave the room.

"Send another girl up here, will ya?" Ben shouted after Jaclyn.

Jaclyn slammed the door of the room and breathed a sigh of relief. Her body felt sticky and she felt nauseous. A good bath will fix her up.

Jaclyn made her way downstairs to the pub where men were drinking and sitting on the floor. Some ladies were on the laps of the men and they cheered as the man drank.

There was a putrid smell in the air as Jaclyn stepped in the room, she gagged at the sight of the pub. She walked up to the pub-tender who smiled at her as she came up to the bar.

"Hello there Jaclyn, how is it going?" the pub-tender John said as Jaclyn sat on a stool.

"I got jilted, that's what is going on," Jaclyn sighed.

"He didn't pay you? No surprise there," John said. "The miners don't get paid till next week."

"So you knew? And you let me go up with him?" Jaclyn asked.

"I knew they didn't get paid but I didn't know he had no money with him," John said.

"I am tired, I just want a bath and a drink to get the taste of Ben out of my mouth."

"He made you—"John angled a brow.

"Yes, John, he made me put my mouth on his miner's dick," Jaclyn said and shuddered.

"Oh, you poor thing," Jack said, he placed a glass in front of Jaclyn and poured alcohol into it. "Drink up," John said.

Jaclyn downed the drink and thanked John. She made her way to the room of Elizabeth, the woman in charge of the prostitution ring in the pub and also Jaclyn's lover.

Jaclyn met Elizabeth in her room, she was writing some letters when Jaclyn came in the room. She stopped at the door when she saw Elisabeth.

Elizabeth was half naked with her breasts in the open while she smoked a cigarette at her table. Jaclyn smiled as she watched Elizabeth work.

"Are you going to come in or you want everyone to see my tits?" Elizabeth yelled from her table.

Jaclyn entered the room and locked the door.

"How did it go today?" Elizabeth asked.

"Very shitty, my first customer didn't pay me and I feel worse than I started," Jaclyn said as she walked to Elizabeth's table.

"Oh your poor thing," Elizabeth said and put out her cigarette.

"I can make you feel better." Elizabeth lifted Jaclyn on the table, Jaclyn giggled as Elizabeth lifted her dress up and started to kiss her thighs.

"Oh you naughty woman," Jaclyn giggled.

"I aim to please," Elizabeth whispered.

She pulled down Jaclyn's undergarment and stuck her face into Jaclyn privates. Jaclyn moaned and held the table as Elizabeth pleasured her.

Afterwards, Elizabeth and Jaclyn relaxed in bed while Jaclyn told Elizabeth about her day

"I hate it here Elizabeth. I hate it more day after day," Jaclyn said, her head was in Elizabeth's lap.

"You can quit you know," Elizabeth said, she was smoking another cigarette.

"I need money to survive Elizabeth," Jaclyn said.

"I have money Jaclyn. I can always give you more than enough."

"I need my own money. I refuse to take money from you."

"What can you do then?"

"I don't know Elizabeth," Jaclyn said starting at the wall. "I really don't know."

CHAPTER TWO

AUGUST 1888

The next day was another day of work for Jaclyn; she downed herself with enough alcohol to numb the disgrace and shame she was feeling. She only had a couple of pounds that day.

Jaclyn knew she deserved better; she used to be a surgical assistant until the police came to arrest the surgeon; he was selling body parts. Jaclyn had to go on the streets, but Elizabeth took her in; she didn't need to sell her body, but Jaclyn offered to do it to pay for her stay at Elizabeth's pub. Jaclyn thought if she made enough money, she would find her way out of London, but she found out she would be stuck in that job. She didn't have enough money saved up.

By the end of the day, Jaclyn was so exhausted that she found her way to the bottom of a whiskey bottle at the bar with Jack. The evenings were usually business for the girls; they went outside on the street to look for customers, men coming home from work who wanted to have a good time before they went home to their wives and kids.

Jackson found her way outside, where some of the other girls were already waiting for customers; Jaclyn staggered to join the girls and tried calling the men going home.

"Hey there, want a quick fuck?" Jaclyn laughed and raised her skirt. Some men looked at her with disgust when some flashed their teeth at her.

Jaclyn looked at the men and turned her head; she deserved better than these men.

"You think you are better than us?"

Jack turned to see another woman standing beside her. Her name was Mary Ann.

"What did you say?" Jaclyn asked.

"I said do you think you are better than us? You think you don't serve this life of sleeping with men?"

"Yes I am," Jaclyn said.

"You think you are better than us because we just sleep around but we are working for our families. We don't mind sleeping with men, what make you think we enjoy this work? We are sad but we do it anyways. So Jaclyn tell me what makes you special?" Mary Ann folded her hand and eyed Jaclyn.

"I have skills, special skills that I can use and get myself a better life."

"Oh you have skills? Use these skills now Jaclyn, because I don't see you getting out of here and having a better life. You think you are better but you are filth like the rest of us are."

Jaclyn thought and realized Mary Ann was right, her skills hadn't taken her anyway, and she was stuck with the girls whether she liked it or not.

"You are right Marry Ann. I am sorry," Jaclyn said.

"That is okay. It is tough on all of us, the only thing we have is each other." Mary Ann smiled.

"Speaking of each other, do you want to go somewhere else?" Jaclyn asked.

"Like where?" Mary Ann said with a twinkle in her eyes.

"Somewhere private where we can be alone," Jaclyn said as she walked to Mary Ann and played with her hair.

Mary Ann giggles as Jaclyn pulled her into an alley. The two women start to kiss under cover of the alley.

Jaclyn starts to take off Mary Ann's clothes as the woman giggles.

"What if Elizabeth finds out, she will have me sent away," Mary Ann half moaned, half talked as Jaclyn took off her undergarments.

"You will not tell Elizabeth, will you?" Jaclyn asked.

"No, of course not." Mary Ann said.

"Okay good," Jaclyn held her head up, "Don't tell Elizabeth and we would keep our little secret,"

"Okay," Mary Ann giggled.

Jaclyn laughed and stuck her face in Mary Ann's genitals; the woman moaned as Jaclyn pleasured her.

Jaclyn held Mary Ann's neck and squeezed.

"Jaclyn, that's a little tight," Mary Ann whimpered.

"But you like it don't you?" Jaclyn said and came up to see Mary Ann.

"Yes, I do," Mary Ann smiled weakly.

"Good," Jaclyn said and started to squeeze Mary's neck. Her hand squeezed tighter around Mary Ann's neck.

Jaclyn felt a poor rush toward her as Mary Ann whimpered in her hands; she was in charge and felt she could do anything to Mary Ann.

"Do you trust me?" Jaclyn whispered in Mary Ann's ears.

Mary Ann nodded weakly, and Jaclyn smiled.

"Then you will know I don't want you to suffer," Jaclyn said and squeezed tighter.

Mary Ann tried to fight, but Jaclyn covered her mouth so she couldn't scream.

Jaclyn kept looking into the terrified eyes of Mary Ann as she slowly died in her hands. As Mary Ann died, Jaclyn laid the body on the ground and stared at it.

"Now you are free. No man can hurt you anymore," Jaclyn said.

She knelt beside Mary Ann and caressed her face.

"I am sorry you didn't get any better in life. You were a beautiful woman who deserves the best."

Jaclyn closed Mary Ann's eyes and took out her surgeon shrapnel she took everywhere with her in case she was in harm's way. Jaclyn tore off Mary Ann's dress in the front and stared at her naked body. She ran her hands across the cold skin of the dead woman.

"Don't worry, I will take care of your heart for you," Jaclyn said.

She stuck the shrapnel in Mary Ann's chest and made a clean cut; she removed her heart and other organs from the woman's chest.

The blood was everywhere, and some got on Jaclyn's clothes. When done, she gathered the organs in her gown and slid out of the alley through the backyards. She snuck until she got to the river and dumped the organs inside the river. She also washed her dress free of the blood and went back to the pub, where she drank the rest of the night away.

CHAPTER THREE

As Jaclyn woke the next morning, she could hear a commotion in the pub below; she put on a dress and rushed down to the pub to meet a small crowd and Elizabeth at their head. There was also a police officer amid the crowd, and he was talking.

Jaclyn leans against a post and listens to the police officer talk.

"We don't know what happened yet, we are going to start any investigation on the murder," the police officer said.

"An investigation? One of my girls gets murdered on the streets, and all you will do is an investigation?" Elizabeth scoffed; she had a cigarette in her hand as usual. She took a big puff of it.

"Elizabeth, we are doing all we can," the officer said.

"All you can? Yeah right, you will go back to that chicken coop you call a station and you will forget about this case. Do you know why officer?"

"No, I don't believe I do," the office started to stammer.

"Of course, you don't. You will abandon this case because the woman who got murdered was a prostitute. She isn't the kind of lady your station deals with; you see us as filth and old hags," Elizabeth spat at the officer, who recoiled.

The crows started to yell at the officer, they started to throw stuff at him while he tries to get them to calm down, but they didn't have it.

"The next time you show your face in here, it better be with the killer of Mary Ann so we can lynch him," Elizabeth said and threw a cigarette at the officer.

The police officer goes out of the door while the crowd scatters.

"Drinks for everyone," Elizabeth announced, and the crowd cheered.

Elizabeth sees Jaclyn leaning against the post and nods at her. Jaclyn walks to meet Elizabeth where she stood. Elizabeth reeked of whiskey.

"Have you been drinking?" Jaclyn asked Elizabeth.

"Of course, I have been drinking, darling," Elizabeth smiled at Jaclyn, who held her breath at the stink. "Oh, come on, darling, give me a kiss," Elizabeth puckered her lips for a kiss, but Jaclyn stepped back.

"You need to rest and stay off the whiskey for at least a week." Jaclyn said.

"Stay off? A jackass killed one of my best girls, most of the girls are scared of working, and some of the customers are scared of coming in. So yeah, business is great," Elizabeth shouted; she staggered as she talked. "Another glass Jack," Elizabeth shouted.

"No you will not have another glass," Jaclyn said.

"She is right, Elizabeth, you need to rest," Jack said. He was seated at the bar.

"You don't know this business, I am trying to provide for these girls and someone just ups and kills one of them. I will drink if I want to and none of you can tell me what to do," Elizabeth said and burped loudly. She fell to the floor in a heap.

"Oh dear God," Jaclyn groaned and called for Jack.

Jaclyn and Jack carried Elizabeth up to her room, Jaclyn stayed with Elizabeth, and she told Jack to get her some tea to help her clear her head.

"Twenty years, I have owned this place," Elizabeth started to say as Jaclyn got her into the bed. "I have ran this place for twenty years, not one of my girls were murdered, why now?" Elizabeth mumbled.

Jaclyn sat on the bed beside Elizabeth and asked herself the same question. Why now? Why has she decided to kill Mary Ann now? She could have done it years earlier, but why now?

"I will tell you why," Elizabeth said; she sounded like she was crying. "That person hates my girls, the work they do, and he is killing them off one after the other," Elizabeth sighed.

"How did you know he was a man?" Jaclyn said.

"Only a man would something as horrible as that. Mary Ann was mutilated, what kind of woman would even do that?"

Jaclyn sat in silence as Elizabeth relaxed. Jaclyn thought about what she did; she didn't feel sorry for killing Mary Ann but instead felt powerful. She held all the cards and could drop them anytime. The girls' life was degrading, and they needed to be released.

Jaclyn knew Mary Ann was free of the life they had; if she had to, she would do it again.

That evening when Elizabeth was sober enough, she asked Jaclyn to go out with her; they took a carriage and walked in the countryside; Elizabeth had a picnic with Jaclyn, and they talked.

"What is the point of all this?" Jaclyn asked as she sipped wine; she hadn't had wine in a long time.

"I had this planned already. I just wanted to tell you how much I love you," Elizabeth said, smiling.

Jaclyn stared blankly at Elizabeth; they hadn't told each other there was love in their relationship; Jaclyn had some affection for Elizabeth, but that was it. She couldn't love her back.

"Are you sure?" Jaclyn mumbled.

"Yes, I am sure," Elizabeth said; she leaned against Jaclyn and laid on her lap. "You love me too right?" Elizabeth whispered.

"Yeah, of course I do," Jaclyn mumbled.

"I knew it," Elizabeth laughed.

As they returned to the pub that evening, Jaclyn knew she didn't love Elizabeth, but she said what Elizabeth wanted to hear. As Jaclyn returned to her room, she knew she was tired of living life to satisfy people; she would do whatever she wanted.

Jaclyn took out a box she kept under her bed; she opened it to see the tools she used as a surgeon assistant.

"This is for me," Jaclyn said as she smiled at the box of tools.

Jaclyn climbed into bed with a smile; this night, she was going to sleep, but tomorrow night, she was going to go out to save another girl from this life.

CHAPTER FOUR

SEPTEMBER 1888

Jaclyn woke up with a little cheer in her day. Everything was back to normal in the pub, and it was business as usual with the girls. That morning, the pub was packed with people; some men came in to see the attraction while others came to gawk.

Jaclyn went down for a drink, where she learnt from Jack that Elizabeth had taken a two-day trip that morning.

"What did you say?" Jaclyn asked as she downed a glass of whiskey.

"She said some relatives of hers died and she needed to visit her family," Jack said.

"Hmm," Jaclyn scoffed.

Jack gave her a knowing look, and Jaclyn returned the look. Elizabeth didn't have any relatives; she had a daughter she went to see on some days of the year. Elizabeth doesn't know it, but everyone at the pub knew about her daughter.

"When will she be back?" Jaclyn asked.

"She said in two days."

"Who is going to be in charge here?" Jaclyn asked.

"Elizabeth put me in charge. You girls don't need someone to be in charge, you pretty much know how things go. Elizabeth just wants me to break up fights and make sure men who don't pay her girls end up on the streets," Jack smiled.

"Elizabeth and protecting her girls," Jaclyn smiled. She downed the rest of her glass.

"You are going at it heavy this morning eh?" Jack asked.

"I need it, Jack, I need it to be able to fuck these smelly men that come in here," Jaclyn said; she dropped her shoulder as she spoke.

"Jaclyn, you can walk out that door, I will not stop you."

"Don't worry about it Jack. I will put a smile on my face and fuck these idiots, I will take their money and have a good time while at it," Jaclyn smiled, raising her head.

"Atta girl," Jack smiled at her.

Jaclyn left the pub and walked to a table where a man sat lonely; he had just finished a bottle of whiskey.

"What's wrong handsome?" Jaclyn said and slid into the seat beside the man.

"My wife left me," the man slurred; he was drunk.

"Oh darling, that is so sad," Jaclyn said and rubbed the man's head.

"I don't know what I am going to do. She took the children too. Me boys, me wonderful boys," the man slurred further.

"I know what you can do," Jaclyn said as she took the man's hand.

"What?' the man looked at Jaclyn.

"You come upstairs with me," Jaclyn whispered; she spoke directly into the man's ears as she used his hand to caress her thighs.

"Okay," the man said; he started to breathe fast.

"I am going to let you fuck me until I am sore all over," Jaclyn whispered. She held the man's hand to her vagina.

"Okay, the man whimpered.

"Let's go," Jaclyn said; she got out of the seat and dragged the man out of his seat; she took him to her room upstairs.

Later that night, Jaclyn went on the street to scope out another one of the girls she would *free*. She separated from the other girls and watched them; she saw a couple of women in one corner and one woman sitting by herself; she looked sad and downcast. Jaclyn smiled; she found her next victim.

Jaclyn walked to the woman and sat beside her.

"What is the matter, honey?" Jaclyn asked; she noticed he had never seen the woman on the street before. Jaclyn realized she was new to the pub.

"I am nervous about sleeping with men," the lady said.

"You are new, aren't you?"

"Yes, I am new here and I am very nervous."

"What is your name?" Jaclyn asked the lady.

"Annie Murray," the lady smiled.

"I understand, the first few days can be hard for the new girls but there is nothing you need to worry about. It is going to be fine," Jaclyn said.

"You really think so?" Annie looked at Jaclyn with tears in her eyes.

"Come here," Jaclyn put a hand around Annie. "It is okay, I have a way to make you feel better," Jaclyn said.

"You do?" Annie asked.

"Of course I do. Come with me," Jaclyn got to her feet and held a hand to Annie.

Annie gave Jaclyn her hand, and Jaclyn led her to a dark corner.

"Just relax, I will make all your troubles go away."

Jaclyn started to kiss Annie, and she kissed her back; Annie moaned as Jaclyn bit her lips. Jaclyn grabbed one of Annie's legs and held it up as she pushed Annie against the wall.

"It is okay, just trust me," Jaclyn broke the kiss and whispered.

Jaclyn put her hand around Annie's neck and kissed her again; this time, the kiss was rough and demanding. Annie tried to pull away, but Jaclyn didn't give her a chance.

Jaclyn kissed her deeper and deeper until Annie didn't notice the hand around her neck had gotten tighter. There was no sound from Annie as Jaclyn squeezed the life out of her. She fell to the ground in a heap.

"Oh darling, you are saved now; you don't need to sleep with men for money", Jaclyn whispered as she laid Annie on the ground. She admired her face for a second; Annie was beautiful, with white skin and black hair.

"What a waste of beauty," Jaclyn sighed.

She took out the surgery tools she hid inside her dress and cut Annie open. Jaclyn took Annie's heart before the other organs in the lady's body.

When she was done, she gathered the organs in her dress and sneaked out of the alley before someone saw what she had done. As Jaclyn snuck away, she heard a distant scream; someone had found Annie's body. Jaclyn smiled as she snuck into the night to the river, where she dumped the woman's organs and washed up.

When she got back to the pub, the police were outside; she sneaked into the pub from the back and went to bed.

CHAPTER FIVE

SEPTEMBER 1888

Word of the murder started to spread, the girls at the pub became more scared, and Elizabeth hired a guard to stay outside the pub whenever the girls were out in the street. Jaclyn loved the terror in town; it stopped business in the pub, so the girls didn't have to do their filthy job.

Jaclyn enjoyed working with Elizabeth to ensure the pub was safe; she took note of Elizabeth's security measures and made a mental note to avoid them. She and Elizabeth haven't had time to talk about their feelings, and she appreciated the distance.

At night, Jaclyn looked at the streets below, and her heart grew happy seeing the empty streets; she knew the streets would be full soon, and everyone would go about their business as if nothing had happened. She knew she couldn't let everyone forget; she needed to save more girls and everyone from realizing they didn't need this job.

She needed to do something fast. Jaclyn knew she had to put fear into the heart of people but in what way? She had already tried killing people, but people didn't seem to fear her, but that wasn't enough.

Jaclyn sat in bed scratching her head, trying to figure out what to do. She sat up in bed as an idea occurred; she remembered her conversation days ago with Elizabeth when Elizabeth said the killer could be a man.

Jaclyn chuckled as she thought of her plan; she would make everyone terrified of the male character she would create. She would give him a name that would terrify everyone on the streets.

"The Killer Jack," Jaclyn said out loud as she thought in her room. "No, that doesn't sound terrifying," Jaclyn said.

She got off her bed and paced the room, "Jack, the killer?" Jaclyn shook her head; it wasn't going to work.

Jaclyn went to her window to overlook the street below; she could hear some people talking while some people walked to their homes.

"Jack the Ripper?" Jaclyn said; she pondered this in her head for a second.

'"That is it," Jaclyn smiled, "I rip people. That is a befitting name for me," Jaclyn said.

Now, she needed to let the whole of London hear her name; she already had a plan for that, too; her plan was simple, she was going to send the police a letter. But she wanted it to be terrifying, so she decided to write in the blood of her next victim and send it to the police as a little gift so they would know it was from her.

"They will be so terrified," Jaclyn laughed.

All she had to do was wait for her next victim; she was going to make it the perfect murder; oh, how exciting it was going to be.

"Rest today, there will be time to free more people," Jaclyn chuckled as she climbed back into her bed.

Over the next days, Jaclyn planned her next move of how she would get the next victim; the next woman was easy to lure away, her name was Elizabeth, the girls called her "Long Liz," she was a tall woman. Elizabeth was bored and needed excitement in her life; it wasn't hard to get her alone.

Jaclyn didn't take long before she killed Elizabeth; she strangled her by the neck and tore her open. This time she took some of Elizabeth's blood in a jar to keep for herself for the letter she was going to write the police.

After that, Jaclyn stopped killing for a week; she expected the people to believe they were safe. Then the rumours started circulating; some people said the police had caught the killer. Some girls said the man they caught was a doctor; some said he was a surgeon with a tan leather apron; Jaclyn enjoyed the gossip.

She decided to strike while the gossip was hot, getting to her jar of blood; Jaclyn realized it was too thick to write a letter with, so she had to use an alternative. One night, Jaclyn sat side her window while the moon illuminated the skies and penned her letter to the police. It went as thus;

Dear Boss,

I keep on hearing the police have caught me, but they won't fix me just yet. I have laughed when they look so clever and talk about being on the right track. That joke about Leather Apron gave me real fits. I am down on whores, and I shan't quit ripping them until I get buckled. Grand work, the last job was. I gave the lady no time to squeal. How can they catch me now? I love my work and want to start again. You will soon hear of me with my funny little games. I saved some of the proper red stuff in a ginger beer bottle over the last job, but it went thick like glue, and I can't use it. Red ink is fit enough; I hope ha. Ha. The next job I do, I shall clip the lady's ears off and send to the police officers just for jolly, wouldn't you? Keep this letter back until I do a bit more work, then give it straight. My knife's so nice and sharp that I want to get to work immediately if I get a chance. Good Luck. Yours truly

Jack the Ripper

Don't mind me giving the trade name.

Wasnt good enough to post this before I got all the red ink off my hands; curse it. No luck yet. They say I'm a doctor now. haha

Jaclyn mailed the letter anonymously; she sneaked away from the pub and took it to the post office. Within three days of her sending the letter, *Jack The Ripper* was on the lips of every Londoner.

Mothers kept their children, and everyone made sure to get home before it got dark.

CHAPTER SIX

SEPTEMBER 1888

The next murder Jaclyn committed was one of the most daring ones she would ever commit. After the letter circulated, everyone was on the edge of their toes. More police and guards were on the streets.

It was getting challenging, and Jaclyn welcomed it; the murders were easy during the first three times.

No one in the pub even raised an eyelid toward her. The police patrolled the area to single out some men that might be suspects, most of the surgeons in the area were under suspicion, and some of their patients didn't want to come in.

The police came in to take in Jack for interrogation because his name resembled the killer's. When the police arrived, Elizabeth and Jaclyn were waiting for them when they entered the pub and walked up to Jack.

"What is the matter?" Elizabeth asked the first officer that stepped forward.

"We are here to take this man for interrogation," the officer said. The second officer took a step back; he was the officer Elizabeth had shouted at on the day of the first murder.

"Why? Has he done anything wrong?" Elizabeth asked the police.

She turned to Jack, who stood behind the bar.

"Did you do anything wrong Jack? And you didn't tell me," Elizabeth gasped.

"None that I know of," Jack said.

"So officer, what did my employee do that you want to take him into custody?" Elizabeth asked the officer.

"We are rounding up suspects for the Jack the Ripper murders and since your bartender has a name like his–,"

"So you came here to arrest him? Because he has a name like his?" Elizabeth laughed.

Jaclyn chuckled on the stool behind her.

"So if let's say the killer is named after the King, would you storm into the palace and arrest the King too?" Elizabeth asked the officer.

"Well…ma'am..," the officer stammered.

"Cats got your tongue eh?" Elizabeth smirked at the officer.

"He isn't following you to your station," Jaclyn said.

"You heard my bosses, I am not leaving," Jack smiled behind the bar.

"You can't do that," the second officer cried.

"Can't do what? What evidence do you have against him?" Jaclyn asked.

"Uhmm—"

"Get out of my pub unless you don't want to get beaten up," Elizabeth said, getting out of her seat; the officers whimpered as she stood.

"You heard the lady, get out," Jack said.

"You don't want to get beaten up by Elizabeth, she has sent men to the hospital and I hear some of them never recovered," Jaclyn said as she left her seat.

The officer stood for a second; then, they dashed to the door.

"And don't come back here unless you have a warranty," Jaclyn shouted as the officer ran out the door.

"That will teach them," Elizabeth said.

"Thank you," Jack said.

"You can thank me by pouring whiskey into my glass," Elizabeth said and sat back in her seat.

"As you wish ma'am," Jack smiled and poured Elizabeth more whiskey.

"You want a drink?" Jack asked Jaclyn, who was still standing.

"No, I want to lay down for a bit," Jaclyn said.

"Okay, then," Jack said.

"You are not coming down with something are you?" Elizabeth asked.

"No, I just feel a bit tired, last night I had to work a triple."

"You sly fox," Elizabeth whistled.

"I will talk to you later, Elizabeth," Jaclyn smiled and walked up to Elizabeth to kiss her.

"Okay," Elizabeth smiled.

She left Jack and Elizabeth at the pub and went to her room. She slept for a while and woke in the evening. She was ready for the next phase of her plan. Her plan was audacious; she slid into a coat with a hood and slipped out the pub's back door.

She walked with a hunch so people wouldn't pay any attention to her; she walked until she got to the square. Jaclyn sat in a corner and tried to beg people for money as she scoped out her next victim.

She saw a few guards and police patrolling the square; one of them even walked up to her where she sat.

"What do you want, you old hag?" One of the guards asked.

"I just wanted some money to buy me dinner," Jaclyn spoke with a croaked voice.

The guard looked at her in disgust and walked on.

Soon the square became crowded with people; Jaclyn searched with her eyes until she found someone. Jaclyn slid into the darkness, took off her hood, and walked into the square towards the woman she chose to be her next victim.

The woman called herself Catherine; she already knew Jaclyn from around and wasn't nervous to talk to her.

Jaclyn and Catherine sneaked off under the eyes of the guards; they made out for a bit until Catherine suggested something a little more daring.

Jaclyn smiled and took out one of the knives under her dress.

"Care for a little knife play?" Jaclyn smirked at Catherine.

Seeing Jaclyn pull out the knife under her dress, Catherine became nervous.

"Do you always carry a knife with you?"

"Since there is a killer on the loose I have to protect myself," Jaclyn smiled.

"Oh," Catherine whispered.

"Unless of course I am the killer," Jaclyn chuckled.

"I think I want to go back now," Catherine said.

"No darling, you don't get to go back forever," Jaclyn said.

She sprang upon Catherine in a second and strangled the poor woman to death.

Jaclyn tore open Catherine and took out her organs; she left Catherine for the police to find her.

Jaclyn put on her coat to conceal the blood; this time, she didn't take all the organs to the river; she kept one souvenir for herself; a kidney.

Jaclyn kept the kidney in a jar under her bed.

"That will a good gift for the police officers who came in here today."

As Jaclyn climbed into bed, she could hear police whistles and clamor of the people. They found her fourth victim.

CHAPTER SEVEN

NOVEMBER 1888

Due to the inability of the police to find Jack The Ripper, some people decided to start to take matters into their hands. They began to light torches and walk the streets at night. They also held vigils, with some men awake till morning in clusters on the streets waiting awake till morning.

The pub was the hub of activities; Elizabeth started having head counts each morning to ensure the girls were safe and complete. She also introduced a set of new rules to the pub.

- No girl was allowed to walk alone; they were to be in a group of two or more.
- Whenever a girl has a customer in her room, another one of the girls would be standing outside the door.
- No more customers after 7 pm.

Some rules restricted Jaclyn, who wanted to free more girls; none of the girls wanted to fool around with her, so Jaclyn stooped asking before the girls got suspicious and reported her to Elizabeth.

Jaclyn and Elizabeth began to spend more time together in the evenings. Jaclyn wasn't allowed to have any customers, and Elizabeth paid her directly from her pocket; she also had to sleep in Elizabeth's room.

"Why do I have to do this?" Jaclyn cried the first night she had to sleep in Elizabeth's room.

"What do you mean why? I am trying to protect my most expensive asset," Elizabeth said; she walked over to Jaclyn to caress her face.

"But won't the other girls feel somehow? I mean I have my room and I am safe in our room," Jaclyn said.

"Such nonsense, the girls can get jealous if they want to. I know you have your room but I will feel better if you were here in my room," Elizabeth explained.

"Why aren't you letting me work like I used to? I am losing out on some good money," Jaclyn said; she shied away from Elizabeth and sat on the bed.

"Do you need more money? I can give you more if you want," Elizabeth said; she walked over to her table, where she kept a money box. She opened it and took out some money.

"Keep your money Elizabeth. I like to work for my money, even if it is just sleeping with men, I take pride in my pay."

"But the money I give you is x3 of that. You don't have to sleep with men," Elizabeth said; she walked to Jaclyn with the money in her hand. "Here, take it," Elizabeth held the money to Jaclyn.

"No Elizabeth, keep it. I am satisfied with the one you gave to me, I will not take any more money from you."

Elizabeth threw the money on the bed and sat beside Jaclyn on the bed.

"Okay, I won't give you more money, I will let you wrok mornings and afternoons but no nights."

'Okay, that is a shit deal, but I will take it," Jaclyn smiled.

"Good girl," Elizabeth smiled and pulled Jaclyn into bed.

Jaclyn lived a couple of regular days at the pub, doing her job and making money. The people relaxed since there have been no new deaths, so the restrictions on movements have been lifted. The girls were doing business till midnight now.

Jaclyn tried to find a victim while balancing Elizabeth looking at her every step; her chance came one afternoon when she was having drinks at the bar. A woman walked into the bar and asked Jack to pour her some whiskey.

"What do you for fun these days?" the woman asked.

"Sorry?" Jaclyn said.

"I said, what do you do for fun these days?" The woman smiled as Jack poured her a drink; she held her glass to her lips as she spoke.

"Oh fun? Do people still do that?" Jaclyn smiled.

"Oh, that's bad," the woman said; she took a sip of her drink and set down her glass. She left her seat and walked to Jaclyn to touch her shoulder. "Well, I am always down for a good time," the woman said.

She walked out of the pub, leaving Jaclyn stunned.

"Who was that?" Jaclyn faced Jack.

"She is one of my regulars," Jack said.

"I meant her name."

"She is Mary Jane, she works one of the pubs on the other side of town," Jack said.

"She seems interesting, I think me and Elizabeth would be interested in having a few drinks with her."

"She seems interesting, some of the men who frequents the pub say she is one of the best girls. I hear she lives on Miller's Court. She even does house calls," Jack said.

"Huh, house calls, that is interesting," Jaclyn said; she continued having drinks, but she couldn't get Mary Jane out of her mind.

Later that evening, Jaclyn snuck out of the pub to visit Mary Jane; she knocked on her front door and smiled at Mary Jane as she opened the door.

"Hello here," Mary Jane smiled.

"Hi,"

"Are you doing to stand there or are you going to come in?" Mary Jane asked and held the door open.

Jaclyn stepped into the apartment while Mary Jane closed the door behind her. Jaclyn looked around the apartment; it was simple; a couple of chairs and a bed were in the room.

"Would you like a drink?" Mary Jane asked Jaclyn.

"I would, thank you," Jaclyn said and took a seat.

Mary Jane poured the drinks in front of Jaclyn and handed her a glass.

'I didn't think you would show up," Mary Jane said as he sat beside Jaclyn.

"I had to. I am one for having fun too," Jaclyn said.

"Oh good," Mary Jane said; she sipped the drink in her hand.

"So most women I know don't have apartments and Jack told me your work history, so how did you get this place?" Jaclyn asked.

"One of my clients gave it to me. It was his wife's but she cheated on him so he came to me, we fucked a few times and he gave me the apartment."

"That pussy must be good," Jaclyn smiled.

"How can you tell until you try it?" Mary Jane chuckled and downed her glass.

CHAPTER EIGHT

"You want me to try out your pussy?" Jaclyn asked Mary Jane.

"You are a straight forward woman," Mary Jane smiled.

"Well why would I come here if you didn't want to me to be straight forward?"

"I like how you think, Miss Jaclyn," Mary Jane said.

"How did you know my name?" Jaclyn asked as Mary Jane leaned over the table to fill her glass.

"You are not stranger to me. I have heard of Elizabeth's eye candy and I wanted to get a taste of what she was enjoying from you," Mary Jane said and relaxed in her seat.

"I am here now Mary Jane. What do you need me to do to you?" Jaclyn asked.

Mary Jane paused and took a sip of her drink.

"Actually I don't need anything."

"I beg your pardon?" Jaclyn asked, visibly shocked.

"I don't need you to do anything to me, for me or anything else," Mary Jane smiled. "I just wanted to meet you and talk to you."

"Oh, okay. I should be leaving then," Jaclyn set down her glass.

"You can leave now but you will come a later date. I don't want to draw attention to you," Mary Jane said.

"Why do you want me to come back?" Jaclyn asked.

"Yes, I want you to come back. I need to have that pussy Elizabeth gushes over," Mary Jane smiled and leans to kiss Jaclyn.

"Wow," Jaclyn said; she was stunned at the kiss.

"Good bye for now, Jaclyn," Mary Jane said.

Jaclyn got out of her chair and went to the door. "When do you want me to come back?" Jaclyn asked at the door.

"You can come by anytime you want, my door will be op to you," Mary Jane smiled.

Jaclyn left Mary Jane's apartment and walked back to the pub; she spent the rest of the evening smiling. Elizabeth noticed and asked her what was going on.

"You seem lively today, Jaclyn; what is the matter?" Elizabeth asked; she and Jaclyn sat down for dinner.

"I am just happy to be doing my job and getting my own money," Jaclyn said, smiling.

"But you say you don't like this job but now you are happy to be doing it?" Elizabeth angled a brow at Jaclyn.

"I don't know. Something is different today, the sky was brighter toddy," Jaclyn laughed.

"Wow, I have never seen you this happy, Jaclyn," Elizabeth said.

"Let's eat, darling, Jaclyn said.

"You never call me darling, something is different," Elizabeth laughed.

"I guess it is your love that is making me extra happy today," Jaclyn said and reached over to grab Elizabeth's hands. "You make me happy Elizabeth and I love how you love me," Jaclyn said.

"Oh Jaclyn," Elizabeth said, smiling as she stared at Jaclyn.

Jaclyn smiled as she lifted a cup of wine to her lips; she was thinking of Mary Jane all the time and couldn't wait till she got to Mary Jane.

Over the next day, Jaclyn planned her next murder; she cleaned her tools because this one would be special for her. She chose a day when no one would suspect her; she made herself scarce and slipped out the back door to go to Mary Jane's apartment, where Mary Jane was waiting for her.

"Hello there," Mary Jane said as she opened the door to Jaclyn, wearing a coat.

Jaclyn walked into the apartment to see that Mary Jane had closed the door and taken off her coat; she was naked under the coat.

"Wow," Jaclyn smiled.

"Let's not waste our time shall we," Mary Jane said and leaped at Jaclyn.

The woman started to kiss, and they ended up on the bed; Jaclyn took off her dress and tossed it on the ground as Mary Jane groped her. They began to have sex, and their moans filled the room.

Afterward, Jaclyn and Mary Jane relaxed in bed naked.

"So that is how you taste like," Jaclyn smiled.

"And that is how you taste like," Mary Jane smiled.

"I feel I could go on and on," Jaclyn said and started biting Mary Jane's neck.

"You are like an animal," Mary Jane chuckled.

"Don't tell me you are tired already?" Jaclyn laughed.

"Oh no darling, I am just getting ready," Mary Jane smiled and cupped Jaclyn's face to kiss her.

Jaclyn kissed her back; she took her hand to Mary Jane's neck.

"Oh, I like that," Mary Jane moaned.

"Then you will love this," Jaclyn said.

Jaclyn tightened her hold on Mary Jane's neck, who was moaning and didn't know what was going on until Jaclyn cut off her air. Mary Jane went limp as life left her body.

Jaclyn smiled at her face. "You are saved."

She went to her dress, where she had taped her tools to her dress before she left the pub; she was naked, so she didn't worry about any blood getting on her. Jaclyn took her time preparing Mary Jane's body for the *surgery*.

She started by cutting Mary Jane open as gently as she could; she wanted the process to last because she wanted to enjoy it.

The whole process of Jaclyn performing surgery took two hours; Jaclyn wore her dress and packed the organs in a small bag she had also taped to her dress.

She slipped out of Mary Jane's apartment, checking to see if no one saw her; as she left, she walked back to the pub to put each of the organs into a jar. It was a souvenir of her most significant kill yet.

Jaclyn went about her activities for the rest of the evening; she even had sex with Elizabeth in the night and told her she loved her.

The following day, talk had circulated the pub, this time, it wasn't one of their girls. It was another woman in her apartment. The people started to rally at the police station.

Jaclyn enjoyed the chaos; they didn't see it coming.

CHAPTER NINE

The people didn't take Mary Jane's death lightly, they had had enough of Jack the Ripper, and the police were under more pressure than ever; the people were demanding answers.

Jaclyn knew she had to lay at an all-time low, the streets were getting crowded, and she couldn't risk being in the open again, not after Mary Jane. The privacy her apartment provided gave Jaclyn the time she needed to think and do a clean surgery. She loved the power she felt when she dug into Mary Jane's chest to caress her heart, the adrenaline she felt as she held the shrapnel to cut. She didn't think she would never feel like that again.

The girls at the pub and some other girls from the other pubs around town decided to hold a wake for Mary Jane; they would walk the streets at night holding candles. Jaclyn agreed to participate in the event even if she didn't want to, but everyone was participating, including Elizabeth.

On the night of the wake, the girls converged at the square where Catherine was found, and they started to walk to Mary Jane's apartment; on their way, they sang songs and talked with each other.

As Jaclyn walked, she noticed a small boy amid the crowd; he had a candle and was crying. Jaclyn walked up to him.

"What are you doing here? Are you not supposed to be asleep?" Jaclyn asked as she crouched to the boy's level.

"I am looking for my mommy?" the boy said; he stared at Jaclyn with his tear-streaked face.

"Your mother is here? We will find her," Jaclyn said. She picked up the boy and put him on her hip.

Jaclyn walked further into the crowd to find the boy's mother; most women said they didn't know who he was. One woman eventually explained whose son he was.

'He is the son of Mary Jane," the woman said, staring at the boy on Jaclyn's hip.

"Mary Jane doesn't have any children," Jaclyn said in disbelief.

"Yes, she has a child. A boy, she doesn't live with him but she has a son and that is him," the woman pointed at the boy.

"Are you talking about my mommy?" the boy asked; he stifled a yawn; he was tired.

Jaclyn glanced at the boy; *what have I done?* Jaclyn thought. The boy needed a home to sleep in, and his mother was dead because she had killed her; the least she could do for him was looking for a place to sleep.

Later that night, Jaclyn bursts through the pub doors with a sleeping boy in her arms. Elizabeth immediately took the child from her and gave him to one of the girls, who went to find a room for him.

"Who was that?" Elizabeth asked Jaclyn. "Do you have a son I do not know about?" Elizabeth joked.

"He was the son of the murdered woman. I don't have time for this," Jaclyn said and stormed off, leaving Elizabeth dazed in her wake.

Jaclyn stormed into her room and locked the door behind her; she went to lay in her bed. As she lay on her bed, she bursts into tears.

Jaclyn felt ashamed of what she had done; she liked killing and freeing these women, but she didn't think about their families or if people would miss them if they died. Mary Jane had a young son who had no one to take care of him.

She understood how it felt without having any parents; she didn't have any parents, and the two died shortly after she was born. She had to live on the streets with a few relatives who didn't care whether she lived or died. Some Catholics took her in and gave her food until she eventually ran away to become a surgeon's assistant. Jaclyn didn't want Mary Jane's son to end up as she did; she would find a way to make this right.

She was going to do something right after a long while, turning herself in so the murders could stop and everyone could have some peace of mind.

Jaclyn decided to write a letter to the police telling them of her identity so they could come and arrest her in front of everyone. She was done.

Jaclyn went to the window in her room to stare at the people still holding candles in the streets below.

I am going to make this right, Jaclyn whispered.

She took a sheet of paper and started to pen her letter to the police; she wanted to make a proper confession.

Dear boss,

As a young child, I was orphaned; I saw enough wrongs and horrible things in the world, and this letter will not discuss them. I am writing this to ensure this kind of event never takes place in London again.

My name is Jack the Ripper; some of you know me as the man who kills and mutilates women; I think of myself as their savior. I am saving them from a life of poverty, anger, and shame. You do not know that most people know me as Jaclyn Herring, a prostitute.

I have seen these women's horrors and am not ashamed of what I did. I freed those women, and I am proud that I did.

Some information has come to light that made me regret my decisions in the first place; I do not regret the murders; I only regret my decision.

I am now confessing to the deaths of Mary Ann Nichols, Annie Chapman, Elizabeth Stride, Catherine Eddowes, and Mary Jane Kelly. I solely carried out those murders, using my skills as a former surgery assistant to harvest organs I dumped in the river.

If you are interested in catching me, I will be at Elizabeth's Pub with a bottle of whiskey; perhaps we can share a bottle before you take me into custody.

For now,

Jaclyn The Ripper.

CHAPTER TEN

Jaclyn stared at the letter she had just written; tears streaked from her eyes; the letter got tear-soaked as she sobbed her heart out. She crumbled the letter in her hand and fell to the floor; she didn't understand what she was doing and was scared of getting arrested.

She knew she would hang; if they didn't hang her, the people would lynch her and publicly burn her. She didn't want to go out that way.

"Oh God, what will I do?" Jaclyn sobbed on the ground. "I am sorry," Jaclyn shouted.

She collapsed and started to roll on the ground. *I know what to do,* Jaclyn thought.

She got off the ground, cleaned the tears, squeezed the letter she wrote, and threw it under her bed. She left her room to get down to the pub. The pub was empty as most of the girls were still out on the street, but Jack was at the pub. Elizabeth was nowhere to be found.

"How are you doing?" Jack asked Jaclyn as she slid into one of the stools. "Have you been crying?"

"No, I have not," Jaclyn said absentmindedly.

"You have been here for about four years Jaclyn and I know when you are lying," Jack said.

"I don't know what to do, Jack," Jaclyn said; she stared at nothing.

"Don't know what to do about what?"

"Everything, I am confused."

"Can you tell me what is going on?" Jack asked.

"Tell me Jack. What do you do when you are in a fix? When you don't know how to move forward?"

"Okay, since I don't know what you are talking about, I will pour you a drink so your head can clear up and you can talk to me."

"Yes, pour me a drink. My last drink," Jaclyn said.

"What do you mean?" Jack asked as she poured Jaclyn a glass.

"Thank you Jack," Jaclyn said and reached for the glass.

"Jaclyn, if you have a problem, all you have to do is talk about it or talk to Elizabeth," Jack said.

"Okay, I will consider it but you didn't answer my questions," Jaclyn said.

"Okay Jaclyn. What I do when I am in a fix is talk to people who can help me. I don't try to run away from the problem."

"What will happen if you run away from the problem?" Jaclyn shrugged.

"You are going to ruin it for yourself and everyone."

"What if I found a way to run away from my problem without ruining it for everyone?"

"You should show me that way then. I would love to know more about it," Jack laughed.

"Maybe I will show you— and everyone," Jaclyn said, drinking the rest of the whiskey in her glass.

"Okay then, we are looking forward to your method," Jack smiled at Jaclyn.

Jaclyn stood from where she was seated and stared at Jack.

"It has been an honor to know you Jack. You are a good man and I hope you get to do great thigs in life," Jaclyn said.

"It has been an honor too?"

"Give my regards to the girls. Tell them I was sorry," Jaclyn smiled sadly.

Jack saw her smile and understood what was going on. "Jaclyn, you don't have to do this."

"It is okay Jack. I am not in any pain," Jaclyn smiled again. She started to walk in the direction of the stairs to get back to her room.

"What about Elizabeth?" Jack called after her. "What do you want me to tell Elizabeth?"

Jaclyn halted in her steps, "Tell her it has been wonderful to be with her. Tell her she is a wonderful woman, and I don't regret anything," Jaclyn said, her voice breaking.

"Are you certain you don't want to tell her that yourself?" Jack asked.

"No, I don't think I can face her like this," Jaclyn turned and started to cry. "I don't want her to know what I am about to do. She will not understand if I talk to her."

"I understand," Jack said and walked to Jaclyn to hug her.

"Oh Jack, I am so scared," Jaclyn sobbed.

"Don't do it then," Jack whispered.

"No, I have to do this," Jaclyn sniffed.

"Okay Jaclyn," Jack released Jaclyn from his hold. "Do what you need to."

Jaclyn nodded at Jack before she started to walk to the stairs. She made it to her room and closed the door behind her, ensuring she locked it. She went to her bed and knelt on the ground. The Catholics who took her in taught her how to pray and knew she needed God's forgiveness more than ever.

Dear God, I seek your forgiveness in my hour of darkness; I know not what I am about to do, but I have committed heinous acts that I cannot be pardoned for.

I look upon you one last time bore I embark on my final journey; I have brought pain to people who did nothing to wrong me. I saw myself as their messiah and savior, but I was wrong.

I pray you to forgive me. I am afraid, God.

Amen.

Jaclyn got off her knees and went to her clothes cupboard, where she took out a piece of rope. She climbed on her bed to tie the rope to a hook on the roof. She started to sob as she slid the noose around her neck.

Jaclyn leaped off the bed with the noose at her neck. She swung limp in the air as life left her and her eyes went lifeless.

The following day, Elizabeth went to Jaclyn's room to get her to have breakfast in her room. As she opened the door, she let out a scream as she saw Jaclyn's body in the air.

"Oh, Jaclyn, Elizabeth said, dropping to the ground in tears.

Jack ran to the room to see what had happened; she held Elizabeth as he stared at Jaclyn's body. "She was brave."

After Jaclyn died, there were no more murders, and London was free.

www.ingramcontent.com/pod-product-compliance
Lightning Source LLC
Chambersburg PA
CBHW070654130626
46555CB00006B/2869